The Book of
Fairy Poetry

The Book of Fairy Poetry

Selected and illustrated by

Michael Hague

HarperCollins Publishers

To My Mother,
The Little Girl from Kensington Gardens,
Daisy Marie King

The Book of Fairy Poetry
Copyright © 2004 by Michael Hague
Manufactured in China by South China Printing Company Ltd.
All rights reserved.
www.harperchildrens.com

Library of Congress Cataloging-in-Publication Data
The book of fairy poetry / selected and illustrated by Michael Hague.
    p. cm.
Summary: A collection of poems about fairies, including selections by William Shakespeare and Jack Prelutsky.
ISBN 0-688-14004-1
1. Fairy poetry, English. 2. Children's poetry, English. [1. Fairies—Poetry. 2. Poetry—Collections.] I. Title.
II. Hague, Michael.
PR1195.F34 M53 2004
821.008'0375—dc21

2001039219

Typography by Jeanne L. Hogle
2 3 4 5 6 7 8 9 10
❖
First Edition

ARTIST'S NOTE

*I*n a very real sense I have been working on this volume of fairy poetry all my life.

When my mother immigrated to America from her English homeland, she brought with her very few possessions. Among the items she could not bring herself to leave behind were her books from childhood. These old companions of my mother's soon became my friends, and my lifelong love for the fairy world began.

I have collected fairy books for nearly half a century, and my passion has never wavered.

For me, creating pictures for this book is as close to illustrator's heaven as I am likely to get. I am very grateful to HarperCollins for this opportunity. I would like especially to thank Meredith Charpentier and Stephen Fraser, who helped make this book a reality.

So, leave behind the land of machines and noise. As you turn the pages of this book, listen instead to the fairy music and make the unseen world of toadstool woods and gossamer wings visible.

Contents

CHAPTER ONE

Where Fairies Dance

Fairy Shoes

The little shoes of fairies are
　So light and soft and small
That though a million pass you by
　You would not hear at all.

— ANNETTE WYNNE

Lullaby for a Fairy Queen

You spotted snakes with double tongue,
  Thorny hedge-hogs, be not seen;
Newts, and blind-worms, do no wrong;
  Come not near our fairy queen.
    Philomel, with melody
    Sing in our sweet lullaby;
Lulla, lulla, lullaby; lulla, lulla, lullaby.
      Never harm
      Nor spell nor charm,
    Come our lovely lady nigh;
    So, good night, with lullaby.

Weaving spiders, come not here;
  Hence, you long-legg'd spinners, hence!
Beetles black, approach not near;
  Worm nor snail, do no offence.
    Philomel, with melody
    Sing in our sweet lullaby;
Lulla, lulla, lullaby; lulla, lulla, lullaby.
      Never harm,
      Nor spell nor charm,
    Come our lovely lady nigh;
    So, good night, with lullaby.

FROM *A MIDSUMMER NIGHT'S DREAM*
—WILLIAM SHAKESPEARE

The Fairies Have Never a Penny to Spend

The fairies have never a penny to spend,
  They haven't a thing put by,
But theirs is the dower of bird and of flower
  And theirs are the earth and the sky.
And though you should live in a palace of gold
  Or sleep in a dried-up ditch,
You could never be poor as the fairies are,
    And never as rich.

Since ever and ever the world began
  They have danced like a ribbon of flame,
They have sung their song through the centuries long
  And yet it is never the same.
And though you be foolish or though you be wise,
  With hair of silver or gold,
You could never be young as the fairies are,
    And never as old.

— ROSE FYLEMAN

Fairies

There are fairies at the bottom of our garden!
  It's not so very, very far away;
You pass the gardener's shed and you just keep straight ahead—
  I do so hope they've really come to stay.
There's a little wood, with moss in it and beetles,
  And a little stream that quietly runs through;
You wouldn't think they'd dare to come merry-making there—
        Well, they do.

There are fairies at the bottom of our garden!
  They often have a dance on summer nights;
The butterflies and bees make a lovely little breeze,
  And the rabbits stand about and hold the lights.
Did you know that they could sit upon the moonbeams
  And pick a little star to make a fan,
And dance away up there in the middle of the air?
        Well, they can.

There are fairies at the bottom of our garden!
  You cannot think how beautiful they are;
They all stand up and sing when the Fairy Queen and King
  Come gently floating down upon their car.
The King is very proud and *very* handsome;
  The Queen—now can you guess who that could be
(She's a little girl all day, but at night she steals away)?
          Well—it's ME!

— R O S E F Y L E M A N

The Elf Toper

Each twilight-come
At beetle-drum
For nectar he a-hunting goes,
The twisted bine
He stoops for wine,
Or sups it fresh from off the rose.

From night to morn
His amber horn
He fills at every honey-fountain,
And draineth up
Each flowery cup
That brims with balm on mead or mountain.

— GEORGE DARLEY

fairies

The fairies, it is said
Drop maple leaves into the stream
To dye their waters red.

— KIKAKU

How to Tell Goblins from Elves

The Goblin has a wider mouth
  Than any wondering elf.
The saddest part of this is that
  He brings it on himself.
For hanging in a willow clump
  In baskets made of sheaves,
You may see the baby goblins
  Under coverlets of leaves.

They suck a pink and podgy foot,
  (As human babies do),
And then they suck the other one,
  Until they're sucking two.
And so it is that goblins' mouths
  Keep growing very round.
So you can't mistake a goblin,
  When a goblin you have found.

— MONICA SHANNON

The Pointed People

I don't know who they are,
But when it's shadow time
In woods where the trees crowd close,
With bristly branches crossed,
From their secret hiding places
I have seen the Pointed People
Gliding through brush and bracken.

Maybe a peakèd cap
Pricking out through the leaves,
Or a tiny pointed ear
Up-cocked, all brown and furry,
From ferns and berry brambles,
Or a pointed hoof's sharp print
Deep in the tufted moss,
And once a pointed face
That peered between the cedars,
Blinking bright eyes at me
And shaking with silent laughter.

—RACHEL FIELD

The Noon Call

Hear the call!
Fays, be still!
Noon is deep
On vale and hill.
Stir no sound
The Forest round!
Let all things hush
That fly or creep,—
Tree and bush,
Air and ground!
Hear the call!
Silence keep!
One and all
Hush and sleep!

—WILLIAM ALLINGHAM

In the Gully Green

When I go down the gully green
  Among the moss and wee ferns,
I try to keep myself unseen
  Beneath the musk and treeferns.
I crouch among the maidenhair
  No bigger than a bunny:
And how the Fairies see me there
  Is really very funny.

I never make the littlest sound,
  I never sing or coo-ee,
Nor touch the Fairies' dancing-ground
  Among the grasses dewy;
I never whistle, "Sweet, sweet, sweet!"
  To hear the wild-birds answer,
Nor stir the bracken with my feet
  To fright a Fairy dancer.

Yet, when I come, the Fairies fly
  On rainbow-winged rosellas,
And all the treeferns standing by
  Put up their green umbrellas;
The toadstools, blue and fawn and rose
  And yellow as canaries,
Their little parasols unclose
  to screen the hidden Fairies.

I often see the Fairy rings
  With dew-drops all aglisten,
And hear the noise of Fairy wings,
  So tiny,—if I listen;
The little leaping creek runs past
  And bubbles o'er with laughter,
To think the Fairies fly too fast
  For me to follow after.

When I go down the gully green,
  As quiet as a possum,
I keep my yellow head unseen
  In golden wattle blossom.
No Fairy on the maidenhair
  More light than I could hover;
And, how the Fairies know I'm there,
  I cannot well discover.

—ANNIE R. RENTOUL

The Fairies Dancing

I heard along the early hills,
　Ere yet the lark was risen up,
Ere yet the dawn with firelight fills
　The night-dew of the bramble-cup,—
I heard the fairies in a ring
　Sing as they tripped a lilting round
Soft as the moon on wavering wing.
　The starlight shook as if with sound,
As if with echoing, and the stars
　Prankt their bright eyes with trembling gleams;
While red with war the gusty Mars
　Rained upon earth his ruddy beams.
He shone alone, low down the West,
　While I, behind a hawthorn-bush,
Watched on the fairies flaxen-tressed
　The fires of the morning flush.
Till, as a mist, their beauty died,
　Their singing shrill and fainter grew;
And daylight tremulous and wide
　Flooded the moorland through and through;
Till Urdon's copper weathercock
　Was reared in golden flame afar,
And dim from moonlit dreams awoke
　The towers and groves of Arroar.

—WALTER DE LA MARE

Sea Fairies

Look in the caves at the edge of the sea
If you seek the fairies of spray,
They thrive in the dampness of sea and tide,
With conch for breakfast and lobsters to ride,
With gulls to fly and tides to boom
And the long, white, wandering waves to roam.
Look in the caves! Look in the caves!
When spray fairies hide they flee for caves!
They capture a starfish and fling him high
Till he hooks on the edge of the cloud-borne sky
And there he'll dry till they fetch him down,
The mischievous fairies that live in the foam,
The wayward, white-winged fairies of spray
That ride green lobsters out of the bay
Then float back in on a horseshoe crab,
Scamper and turn and dash for their caves,
Swept by the waves.
Look in the caves! Look in the caves!

— PATRICIA HUBBELL

Overheard on a Saltmarsh

Nymph, nymph, what are your beads?

Green glass, goblin. Why do you stare at them?

Give them me.

        No.

Give them me. Give them me.

               No.

Then I will howl all night in the reeds,
Lie in the mud and howl for them.

Goblin, why do you love them so?

They are better than stars or water,
Better than voices of winds that sing,
Better than any man's fair daughter,
Your green glass beads on a silver ring.

Hush I stole them out of the moon.

Give me your beads, I desire them.

            No.

I will howl in a deep lagoon
For your green glass beads, I love them so.
Give them me. Give them.

        No.

— HAROLD MONRO

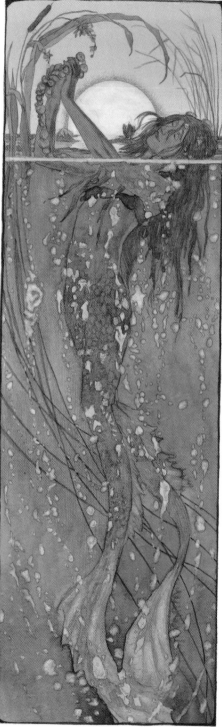

Fairy Washing

The fairies hung their washing out,
  Their linens and their laces,
And some of them were raggedy
  And very torn in places.

But busy old Dame Spider
  Brought out her silver thread
And darned each dainty tablecloth
  And mended every spread.

The fairies were so happy
  They said, "You dear old spinner!
We'll set the toadstool table now
  And you must stay for dinner."

— ROWENA BENNETT

Fairy Fashion

They may take strange
Forms, but never say
They can't be seen—
Only they have a way
Of rearranging things,
Of fitting together
Cold lily-silver
Bodies and dark-netted
Dragonfly wings,

A way of using roses
For faces, dew-
Globes for eyes, and
Spider-silks for hair—
Even their clothing of
Faint moonlight is no
Disguise, but just
The common fashion
All the garden wears.

—VALERIE WORTH

The Ruin

When the last colours of the day
Have from their burning ebbed away,
About that ruin, cold and lone,
The cricket shrills from stone to stone;
And scattering o'er its darkened green,
Bands of the fairies may be seen,
Chattering like grasshoppers, their feet
Dancing a thistledown dance round it:
While the great gold of the mild moon
Tinges their tiny acorn shoon.

— WALTER DE LA MARE

She

In the darkest part of the forest's heart,
in the bowels of a stunted tree,
dwells the fairy fair with fiery hair
who bears the name of SHE.

she is rare of face, with an airy grace,
but evil fills her breast,
by day she sleeps, by night she creeps,
and the forest knows no rest.

when the black bats fly through the cold night sky
she leaves her bed of ferns,
and softly moves on cloven hooves,
as the earth beneath her burns.

when the fairy folk, those wisps of smoke
who flit about the flowers,
sit in the shade of a green grass glade,
they whisper of her powers.

they sit and tell of the evil spell
that turned her soul to stone,
and drove their queen of the fairy green
to the deep dark woods alone.

now evermore on forest floor
the star-crossed fairy flows,
her fiery eyes slay butterflies
and still the fragrant rose.

do not go near this forest drear
where lives no bird or bee,
beware! beware! of the fairy fair
who bears the name of SHE.

— JACK PRELUTSKY

The Kelpie

I was a wayward Kelpie child,
I tossed my elf-locks black and wild;
  No Alphabet knew I!
But I knew the strange and secret things
Of silver fins and downy wings
  And furry creatures sly.

I was a Kelpie child earth-born,
In mortal-land forgot, forlorn;
  My Fairy wings were bound.
But I heard a croon from the wandering moon:
"Come, follow me, follow me, fast and soon!"
  And the moon was full and round.

I heard the white midsummer moon:
"Come, follow! Come, follow!" A Fairy croon!
  My pointed ears I pricked.
I hied me high to the blossomy lea;
the drowsy daisies blinked to see,
  as over the moon I kicked

I kicked above the milk-white moon;
The round world seemed to reel and swoon;
  And free, and free, am I!
I ride on the rack of the storm-cloud's back;
And earth, like a whip-top, small and black;
  Spins fretful in the sky.

—ANNIE R. RENTOUL

The Toadstool Wood

The toadstool wood is dark and mouldy,
　And has a ferny smell.
About the trees hangs something quiet
　And queer—like a spell.

Beneath the arching sprays of bramble
　Small creatures make their holes;
Over the moss's close green velvet
　The stilted spider strolls.

The stalks of toadstools pale and slender
　That grow from that old log,
Bars they might be to imprison
　A prince turned to a frog.

There lives no mumbling witch nor wizard
　In this uncanny place,
Yet you might think you saw at twilight
　A little, crafty face.

—JAMES REEVES

The Ancient Elf

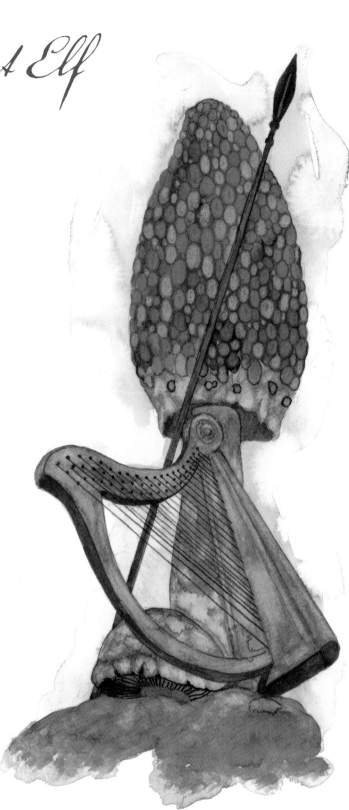

I am the maker,
The builder, the breaker,
The eagle-winged helper,
The speedy forsaker!

The lance and the lyre,
The water, the fire,
The tooth of oppression,
The lip of desire!

The snare and the wing,
The honey, the sting!
When you seek for me—look
For a different thing.

I, careless and gay,
Never mean what I say,
For my thoughts and my eyes
Look the opposite way!

—JAMES STEPHENS

The Little Elf

I met a little Elfman once,
  Down where the lilies blow.
I asked him why he was so small,
  And why he didn't grow.

He slightly frowned, and with his eye
  He looked me through and through—
"I'm quite as big for me," said he,
  "As you are big for you!"

—JOHN KENDRICK BANGS

Over Hill, Over Dale

Over hill, over dale,
  Thorough bush, thorough brier,
Over park, over pale,
  Thorough flood, thorough fire:
I do wander everywhere,
Swifter than the moones sphere;
And I serve the fairy queen,
To dew her orbs upon the green.

The cowslips tall her pensioners be;
In their gold coats spots you see;
Those be rubies, fairy favours,
In those freckles live their savours:
I must go seek some dew-drops here,
And hang a pearl in every cowslip's ear.

FROM *A MIDSUMMER NIGHT'S DREAM*
—WILLIAM SHAKESPEARE

The Fairies' Song

We dance on hills above the wind,
And leave our footsteps there behind;
Which shall to after ages last,
When all our dancing days are past.

Sometimes we dance upon the shore,
To whistling winds and seas that roar;
Then we make the wind to blow,
And set the seas a-dancing too.

The thunder's noise is our delight,
And lightnings make us day by night;
And in the air we dance on high,
To the loud music of the sky.

About the moon we make a ring,
And falling stars we wanton fling,
Like squibs and rockets for a toy;
While what frights others is our joy.

But when we'd hunt away our cares
We boldly mount the galloping spheres;
And, riding so from east to west,
We chase each nimble zodiac beast.

Thus, giddy grown, we make our beds,
With thick, black clouds to rest our heads,
And flood the earth with our dark showers,
That did but sprinkle these our bowers.

Thus, having done with orbs and sky,
Those mighty spaces vast and high,
Then down we come and take the shapes,
Sometimes of cats, sometimes of apes.

Next, turned to mites in cheese, forsooth,
We get into some hollow tooth;
Wherein, as in a Christmas hall,
We frisk and dance, the devil and all.

Then we change our wily features
Into yet far smaller creatures,
And dance in joints of gouty toes,
To painful tunes of groans and woes.

—ANONYMOUS

A Fairy Went A-Marketing

A fairy went a-marketing—
  She bought a little fish;
She put it in a crystal bowl
  Upon a golden dish.
An hour she sat in wonderment
  And watched its silver gleam,
And then she gently took it up
  And slipped it in a stream.

A fairy went a-marketing—
  She bought a coloured bird;
It sang the sweetest, shrillest song
  That ever she had heard.
She sat beside its painted cage
  And listened half the day,
And then she opened wide the door
  And let it fly away.

A fairy went a-marketing—
　She bought a winter gown
All stitched about with gossamer
　And lined with thistledown.
She wore it all the afternoon
　With prancing and delight,
Then gave it to a little frog
　To keep him warm at night.

A fairy went a-marketing—
　She bought a gentle mouse
To take her tiny messages,
　To keep her tiny house.
All day she kept its busy feet
　Pit-patting to and fro,
And then she kissed its silken ears,
　Thanked it, and let it go.

— R O S E   F Y L E M A N

CHAPTER TWO

Fairy Justice

I'd Love to Be a Fairy's Child

Children born of fairy stock
Never need for shirt or frock,
Never want for food or fire,
Always get their heart's desire:
Jingle pockets full of gold,
Marry when they're seven years old.
Every fairy child may keep
Two strong ponies and ten sheep;
All have houses, each his own,
Built of brick or granite stone;
They live on cherries, they run wild—
I'd love to be a Fairy's child.

— R O B E R T   G R A V E S

Scottish Folk Poem

Gin ye ca' me imp or elf,

I rede ye look weel to yourself;

Gin ye ca' me fairy,

I'll work ye muckle tarrie;

Gin guid neibour ye ca' me,

Then guid neibour I will be;

But gin ye ca' me seelie wicht,

I'll be your freend baith day and nicht.

— ANONYMOUS

Seelie means "blessed."

The Leprechaun

In a shady nook one moonlight night,
  A leprechaun I spied
In scarlet coat and cap of green,
  A cruiskeen by his side.
'Twas tick, tack, tick, his hammer went,
  Upon a weeny shoe,
And I laughed to think of a purse of gold,
  But the fairy was laughing too.

With tiptoe step and beating heart,
    Quite softly I drew nigh.
There was mischief in his merry face,
    A twinkle in his eye;
He hammered and sang with tiny voice,
    And sipped the mountain dew;
Oh! I laughed to think he was caught at last,
    But the fairy was laughing too.

As quick as thought I grasped the elf,
    "Your fairy purse," I cried,
"My purse?" said he, "'tis in her hand,
    That lady by your side."
I turned to look, the elf was off,
    And what was I to do?
Oh! I laughed to think what a fool I'd been,
    And the fairy was laughing too.

— ROBERT DWYER JOYCE

Song

We, that are of purer fire,

Imitate the starry quire,

Who, in their nightly watchful spheres,

Lead in swift round the months and years.

The sounds and seas, with all their finny drove,

Now to the moon in wavering morrice move;

And on the tawny sands and shelves

Trip the pert fairies and the dapper elves,

By dimpled brook and fountain-brim,

The wood-nymphs, decked with daisies trim,

Their merry wakes and pastimes keep:

What hath night to do with sleep?

—JOHN MILTON

A Fairy Revel, Before the Coming of Guinevere

He said

That as he rode, an hour or maybe twain

After the sunset, down the coast, he heard

Strange music, and he paused, and turning—there

All down the lonely coast of Lyonnesse,

Each with a beacon-star upon his head,

And with a wild sea-light about his feet,

We saw them—headland after headland flame

Far on into the rich heart of the west:

And in the light the white mermaiden swam

And strong man-breasted things stood from the sea

And sent a deep sea-voice thro' all the land

To which the little sloes of chasm and cleft

Made answer, sounding like a distant horn.

So said my father—yea, and furthermore,
Next morning, while he past the dimlit woods
Himself beheld three spirits mad with joy
Come dashing down on a tall wayside flower
That shook beneath them, as the thistle shakes
When three gray linnets wrangle for the seed:
And still at evenings on before his horse
The flickering fairy-circle wheeled and broke
Flying, for all the land was full of life.
And when at last he came to Camelot,
A wreath of airy dancers hand in hand
Swung round the lighted lantern of the hall;
And in the hall itself was such a feast
As never man had dreamed; for every knight
Had whatsoever meat he longed for served
By hands unseen: and even as he said
Down in the cellars merry bloated things
Shoulder'd the spigot, straddling on the butts
While the wine ran; so glad were spirits and men
Before the coming of the sinful Queen.

—ALFRED, LORD TENNYSON

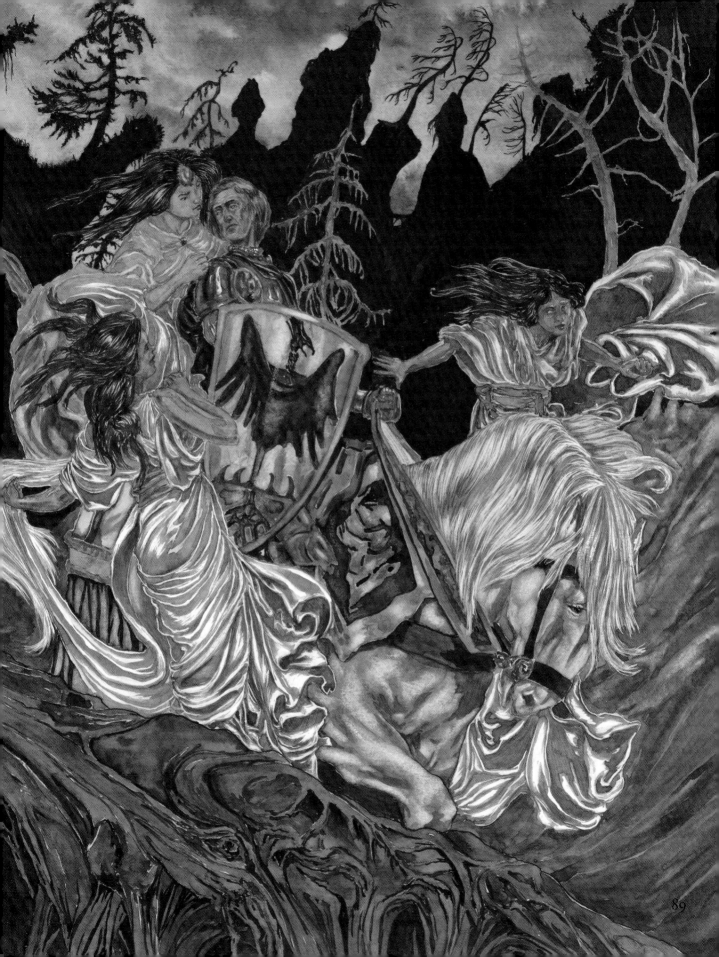

Fairy Song

What I am I must not show—
What I am thou couldst not know—
Something betwixt heaven and hell—
Something that neither stood nor fell—
Something that through thy wit or will
May work thee good—may work thee ill.
Neither substance quite, nor shadow,
Haunting lonely moor and meadow,
Dancing by the haunted spring,
Riding on the whirlwind's wing;
Aping in fantastic fashion
Every change of human passion,
While o'er our frozen minds they pass,
Like shadows from the mirror'd glass.
Wayward, fickle, is our mood,
Hovering betwixt bad and good,
Happier than brief-dated man,
Living ten times o'er his span;
Far less happy, for we have
Help nor hope beyond the grave!

— SIR WALTER SCOTT

The Fairy Queen

Come, follow, follow me,
You, fairy elves that be;
Which circle on the greene,
Come follow Mab, your queene.
Hand in hand let's dance around,
For this place is fairy ground.

—ANONYMOUS

CHAPTER THREE

The Road to Fairyland

The Road to Fairyland

Do you seek the road to Fairyland?
  I'll tell; it's easy, quite.
Wait till a yellow moon gets up
  O'er purple seas by night,
And gilds a shining pathway
  That is sparkling diamond bright.
Then, if no evil power be nigh
  To thwart you, out of spite,
And if you know the very words
  To cast a spell of might,
You get upon a thistledown,
  And, if the breeze is right,
You sail away to Fairyland
  Along this track of light.

— ERNEST THOMPSON SETON

The Nix

The crafty Nix, more false than fair,
  Whose haunt in arrowy Isa lies,
She envied me my golden hair,
  She envied me my azure eyes.

The moon with silvery ciphers traced
  The leaves, and on the waters play'd;
She rose, she caught me round the waist,
  She said, "Come down with me, fair maid."

She led me to her crystal grot,
  She set me in her coral chair,
She waved her hand, and I had not
  Or azure eyes or golden hair.

Her locks of jet, her eyes of flame
  Were mine, and hers my semblance fair;
"O make me, Nix, again the same,
  O give me back my golden hair!"

She smiles in scorn, she disappears,
  And here I sit and see no sun,
My eyes of fire are quenched in tears,
  And all my darksome locks undone.

— R. GARNETT

Elfin Town

I saw the roofs of Elfin Town
  All peaked and pointed gay,
And scores of Elfin chimney-pots
  Smoke-wreathed in blue or gray:
While higher than the Elfin eaves
  Grew shady clover trees,
Some red, some white, but all a-stir
  With humming, gold-winged bees.
I saw the lawns all bright with dew,
  The Elfin windows shine,
And frocks of greenest gossamer
  Hung on a cobweb line.
I heard the tread of Elfin feet;
  A spinning-wheel's soft whirring,
And kettles on an Elfin fire
  Make low and pleasant purring.
From grassy pastures round about
  The bells of Elfin sheep
Went tinkle-tankle drowsily
  From steep to sunny steep.
And sweetly Elfin fiddles scraped,
  And clearly shrilled the horn:—
"Child, Child, come back to Elfin Town
  For it's here that you were born!"

— RACHEL FIELD

102

Mider's Song

How beautiful they are,
The lordly ones
Who dwell in the hills,
In the hollow hills.

They have faces like flowers
And their breath is wind
That blows over grass
Filled with dewy clover.

Their limbs are more white
Than shafts of moonshine:
They are more fleet
Than the March wind.

They laugh and are glad
And are terrible:
When their lances shake
Every green reed quivers.

How beautiful they are,
How beautiful,
The lordly ones
In the hollow hills.

I would go back
To the Country of the Young;
And see again
The lances of the Shee,

As they keep their hosting
With laughing cries
In pale places
Under the moon.

— FIONA MACLEOD

Goblin Stairs

Goblin wood has creepy stairs
  And wisty ti-tree thickets,
And Goblin men as shy as hares,
  And chirpy-brown as crickets.

I put on my scarlet coat.
  And scarlet cap-a-bobbin.
For, if they see me there, I thought,
  They'll take me for a robin.

Down the Goblin stairs I fled
  To see the Goblin people,
The little men in caps of red,
  As peaky as a steeple.

Goblin wood has Goblin snares
  An Goblin ti-tree in it.
When I went down the Goblin stairs,
  I didn't stay a minute.

—ANNIE R. RENTOUL

{from} The Kelpie of Corrievreckan

He mounted his steed of the water clear,
And sat on his saddle of sea-weed sere;
He held his bridle of strings of pearl,
Dug out of the depths where the sea-snakes curl.

He put on his vest of the whirlpool froth,
Soft and dainty as velvet cloth,
And donn'd his mantle of sand so white,
And grasp'd his sword of the coral bright.

And away he gallop'd, a horseman free,
Spurring his steed through the stormy sea,
Clearing the billows with bound and leap
Away, away, o'er the foaming deep!

—CHARLES MACKAY

Little John Bottlejohn

Little John Bottlejohn lived on a hill,
  And a blithe little man was he.
And he won the heart of a pretty mermaid
  Who lived in the deep blue sea.
And every evening she used to sit
  And sing by the rocks of the sea,
"Oh! little John Bottlejohn, pretty John Bottlejohn,
  Won't you come out to me?"

Little John Bottlejohn heard her song,
  And he opened his little door,
And he hopped and he skipped, and he skipped and he hopped,
  Until he came down to the shore.
And there on the rocks sat the little mermaid,
  And still she was singing so free,
"Oh! little John Bottlejohn, pretty John Bottlejohn,
  Won't you come out to me?"

Little John Bottlejohn made a bow,
 And the mermaid, she made one, too;
And she said, "Oh I never saw anyone half
 So perfectly sweet as you!
In my lovely home 'neath the ocean foam,
 How happy we both might be!
Oh! little John Bottlejohn, pretty John Bottlejohn,
 Won't you come down with me?"

Little John Bottlejohn said, "Oh yes!
 I'll willingly go with you,
And I never shall quail at the sight of your tail,
 For perhaps I may grow one, too."
So he took her hand, and he left the land,
 And plunged in the foaming main.
And little John Bottlejohn, pretty John Bottlejohn,
 Never was seen again.

— LAURA E. RICHARDS

The Fairy Boy

A little Fairy in a tree
Wrinkled his wee face at me:
And he sang a song of joy
All about a little boy,
Who upon a winter night,
On a midnight long ago,
Had been wrapt away from sight
Of the world and all its woe:
Wrapt away,
Snapt away
To a place where children play
In the sunlight every day.
Where the winter is forbidden,
Where no child may older grow,
Where a flower is never hidden
Underneath a pall of snow;
Dancing gaily
Free from sorrow,
Under dancing summer skies,
Where no grim mysterious morrow
Ever comes to terrorise.

— MOIRA O'NEILL

CHAPTER FOUR

Tairy Helpers

The Fairy Man

It was, it was a fairy man
  Who came to town to-day;
"I'll make a cake for sixpence
  If you will pay, will pay."

I paid him with a sixpence,
  And with a penny too;
He made a cake of rainbows,
  And baked it in the dew.

The stars he caught for raisins,
  The sun for candied peel,
The moon he broke for spices
  And ground it on a wheel.

He stirred the cake with sunbeams,
  And mixed it faithfully
With all the happy wishings
  That come to you and me.

He iced it with a moonbeam,
  He patterned it with play,
And sprinkled it with star dust
  From off the Milky Way.

— MARY GILMORE

119

The Second-Hand Shop

1

Down in the grasses
Where the grasshoppers hop
And the katydids quarrel
And the flutter-moths flop—
Down in the grasses
Where the beetle goes "plop,"
An old withered fairy
Keeps a second-hand shop.

2

She sells lost thimbles
For fairy milk pails
And burnt-out matches
For fence posts and rails.
She sells stray marbles
To bowl on the green,
And bright scattered beads
For the crown of the queen.

3

Oh, don't feel badly
Over things that you lose
Like spin tops or whistles
Or dolls' buckled shoes;
They may be the things that
Fairy folk can use,
For down in the grasses
Where the grasshoppers hop
A withered old fairy
Keeps a second-hand shop.

— Rowena Bennett

Wind in the Ti-Tree

Up in the ti-tree hid from view
   A little Fairy sings to me;
Her hair is gold, her eyes are blue,
   Like Summer sun and Summer sea.
Her voice is full of singing sails
   And singing shells and singing birds;
And I can hear the Fairytales
   She murmurs low in Fairy words.

They say my Fairy sweet and shy
   Is wind among the ti-tree boughs;
But once I climbed so high, so high,
   And saw the Fairy in her house.
She showed me cradled silver-eyes
   All in a green and mossy nest,
And I could almost touch the skies
   And brush the passing seagull's breast.

Through branchy peep-holes in the tree
  I saw the blue-eyed waves below;
And, while my Fairy sang to me,
  The East wind rocked us to and fro.
I saw the Mermaids in the foam
  Clap their white hands and shout in mirth;
And, oh, I loved the Fairy's home
  So close to Heaven, so close to Earth.

Sometimes the little Fairy sleeps;
  The wind rocks hushabye no more;
A star, to be her candle, peeps
  Among the ti-tree by the shore.
But in the morning on the sand
  Her Fairy music comes awake;
She stays away from Fairyland
  All for a little Earth-child's sake.

—ANNIE R. RENTOUL

Foam Fairies

One where the wave breaks,
 Where I love to play,
The little white Foam Fairies
 Came dancing in the spray,
Little wild Foam Fairies
 Leaping in the air;
Sea-green their eyes were,
 Kelpy-brown their hair.

Up in the little pools,
 Crawling quite alone,
I nearly caught a baby one
 All to be my own.
Out of the big sky,
 Glimmery and gay,
A wicked little star popped,
 And frightened it away.

In the morning early,
 At the peep of sun,
The little white Foam Fairies
 Had vanished every one.
Just a broken necklace
 On the shore was tossed,
A little fringe of pinky shells
 The baby one had lost.

—ANNIE R. RENTOUL

The Gnome

I saw a gnome
As plain as plain
Sitting on top
Of a weathervane.

He was dressed like a crow
In silky black feathers,
And there he sat watching
All kinds of weathers.

He talked like a crow too,
Caw caw caw,
When he told me exactly
What he saw,

Snow to the north of him
Sun to the south,
And he spoke with a beaky
Kind of a mouth.

But he wasn't a crow,
that was as plain as plain
'Cause crows never sit
On a weathervane.

What I saw was simply
A usual gnome
Looking things over
On his way home.

— HARRY BEHN

Gossip

"Trains are all the fashion,"
  Said the fairy in the tree.
"They'll catch upon the brambles
When we go for moonlight scrambles,
  And then where shall we be?"

"At the caterpillar's wedding,"
Said the pixie in the moss,
"The dewdrops were so fizzy
That all the guests went dizzy.
The Queen was very cross."

"The weather clerk's gone crazy,"
Said the brownie in the fern,
"And all the kinds of weather
Have got mixed up together.
They don't know where to turn!"

"It's nothing else but temper,"
  Said the nixie in the pool;
"They've hung him on a spire
With a little bit of wire
  And left him there to cool."

"But have you heard the latest?"
  Said the goblin in the ditch.
"Young Puck has changed the dresses
Of the little twin princesses,
  And they don't know which is which!"

— ROSE FYLEMAN

A Singing Lesson

Greenish frog with mottled throat,
Little imp in speckled coat,
    I will teach you how to sing
      In a Fairy way.
Sing in drip-drop water-notes,
Lightly as a lily floats,
    Softly as the rushes swing
      On a Summer day.

Mortal songs are loud and rough,
Never sweet and low enough;
      Mortals never hear the Moon
         Singing to the Sea.
Mortals stretch their mouths to O,
Shouting fiercely words like "Do";
      Mortals could not hear a croon
         Sung by you and me.

Greenish frog, you must not croak;
Such are sounds for mortal folk.
      I will teach you Fairy bars
         By the Fairies sung.
Little imp, you squeak away
Like a bat at close of day.
      Little mouths should sing like stars,
         When the dawn is young.

—ANNIE R. RENTOUL

The Elfin Pedlar

Lady and gentlemen fays, come buy!
No pedlar has such a rich packet as I.

Who wants a gown
  Of purple fold,
Embroidered down
  The seams with gold?
    See here!—a Tulip richly laced
    To please a royal fairy's taste!

Who wants a cap
    Of crimson grand?
By great good hap
    I've one on hand:
        Look, sir!—a Cock's-comb, flowering red,
        'Tis just the thing, sir, for your head!

Who wants a frock
    Of vestal hue?
Or snowy smock?—
    Fair maid, do you?
        O me!—a Ladysmock so white!
        Your bosom's self is not more bright!

Who wants to sport
    A slender limb?
I've every sort
    Of hose for him:
        Both scarlet, striped, and yellow ones:
        This Woodbine makes such pantaloons!

Who wants—(hush! hush!)
    A box of paint?
'Twill give a blush
    Yet leave no taint:
        This Rose with natural rouge is fill'd,
        From its own dewy leaves distill'd.

Then lady and gentlemen fays, come buy!
You never will meet such a merchant as I!

—GEORGE DARLEY

Ariel's Song

Come unto these yellow sands,
And then take hands;
Curtsied when you have, and kissed
The wild waves whist,
Foot it featly here and there,
And, sweet sprites bear
The burden. Hark, hark!

FROM *The Tempest*
—WILLIAM SHAKESPEARE

Puck's Blessing

Through the house give glimmering light
 By the dead and drowsy fire;
Every elf and fairy sprite
 Hop as light as bird from brier;
And this ditty after me
Sing, and dance it trippingly.

First, rehearse your song by rote,
To each word a warbling note;
Hand in hand, with fairy grace,
Will we sing, and bless this place.

FROM *A MIDSUMMER NIGHT'S DREAM*
—WILLIAM SHAKESPEARE

Index of Titles

Index of Authors

Index of First Lines

Acknowledgments

Grateful acknowledgment is made to the authors and publishers for the use of the following material. Every effort has been made to contact original sources. If notified, the publishers will be pleased to rectify an omission in future editions.

"Elfin Town," by Rachel Field. From *Poems*, by Rachel Field. Reprinted with the permission of Simon & Schuster Books for Young People, an imprint of Simon and Schuster Children's Publishing Division. Copyright 1926 Macmillan Publishing Company; copyright renewed 1954 Arthur S. Pederson.

"The Fairies Dancing," by Walter de la Mare. From *Down-Adown-Derry*, by Walter de la Mare, copyright 1922 by Constable & Company. Used by permission of The Literary Trustees of Walter de la Mare and the Society of Authors as their representative.

"Fairy Fashion," by Valerie Worth. From *Fairy Poems*, edited by Daisy Wallace, Holiday House, copyright 1980. Reprinted by permission of George W. Bahlke.

"The Gnome," by Harry Behn. From *Windy Morning*, by Harry Behn. Copyright 1953 Harry Behn. Copyright renewed 1981 by Alice Behn Goebel, Pamela Behn Adam, Prescott Behn, and Peter Behn. Used by permission of Marian Reiner.

"How to Tell Goblins from Elves," by Monica Shannon. From *Goose Grass Rhymes*, by Monica Shannon, copyright 1930 by Doubleday, a division of Random House, Inc. Used by permission of Doubleday, a division of Random House, Inc.

"I'd Love to Be a Fairy's Child," by Robert Graves. From *Fairies and Fusiliers*, by Robert Graves, 1917. Used by permission of Carcanet Press Limited.

"Overheard on a Saltmarsh," by Harold Monro. From *The Silent Pool*, by Harold Monro, copyright 1942. Reprinted by permission of Gerald Duckworth & Co. Ltd.

"The Pointed People," by Rachel Field. From *Poems*, by Rachel Field. Reprinted with the permission of Simon & Schuster Books for Young People, an imprint of Simon and Schuster Children's Publishing Division. Copyright 1924 Macmillan Publishing Company; copyright renewed 1952 Arthur S. Pederson.

"The Ruin," from *Peacock Pie*, by Walter de la Mare. Used by permission of The Literary Trustees of Walter de la Mare and the Society of Authors as their representative.

"Sea Fairies," by Patricia Hubbell. From *8 A.M. Shadows*, by Patricia Hubbell. Copyright 1965, 1993 by Patricia Hubbell. Used by permission of Marian Reiner for the author.

"She," by Jack Prelutsky. From *Fairy Poems*, edited by Daisy Wallace, Holiday House, copyright 1980. Used by permission of Jack Prelutsky.